STRANGE THOUGHTS

STRANGE THOUGHTS

DEJAN STOJANOVIĆ

New Avenue Books

New Avenue Books

First Edition

Library of Congress Control Number: 2025936554

ISBN-13: 978-1-966571-20-9

NOTE TO THIS EDITION

This book includes prose poems, short stories, epigrams, aphorisms, vignettes, and mini-essays originally written in English between 2005 and 2010, with a few exceptions that were added or corrected later. The last essay was written recently.

D. S.

Contents

MASTERFUL ILLUSION

I am the one who exists yet does not exist,
Who believes he is real even while knowing he is not.

I am the one who flew to the end of emptiness and returned,
All while remaining in the same place.

I am the one who kissed the darkness with lips of light
And embarked on a cosmic journey to conquer darkness.

I am the one whose tears went unseen—
Tears that sank into emptiness, swallowing it whole.

I am the one who transformed unbearable nothingness
Into the most masterful illusion called the Universe,

The tears of the unborn world carried me on their wings into life,
Into the creation of the magnificent Home of Infinity.

The world endures, and I cry tears of happiness in it,
Spreading light all over the Cosmic Home of All.

PROSE POEMS AND STORIES

STONE OF KNOWLEDGE

No Stone of knowledge truly exists. The world is the only source of knowledge. Is it God's Stone, or is God the only Stone? The answer may seem less important than the fact that the Stone exists. We can feel it and see it.

This Stone is alive; it is a massive brain, a vast library, a wild yet tamed animal, all simultaneously. It is its ancestor and descendant, embodying a source, harbor, memory, and reverie. It stands as a volcanic island of existence in the vacuum of emptiness; it writes and erases itself, finding its place in the long history of awakenings and rebirths. It is both the beginning and the end, its cause and purpose.

There is no space, no time, and no matter. This Stone may appear made of matter, but it is not; it is knowledge. We are part of that knowledge—letters of its alphabet, numbers, and notes in a never-ending symphony of thoughts.

The whole world is a thought—a Stone of knowledge searching for purpose. We are all thoughts surrounded by thoughts and programs within a larger program. Our senses decode what appears to be matter, yet they are all part of the immaterial Stone of Knowledge.

SOUL OF THE WORLD

That was yet another carefully crafted joke meant to divert attention and obscure the truth. I turn off the TV, with its parade of new magicians, purveyors of happiness, and doctors eager to heal the soul while knowing little about it. Sometimes, I close my eyes and ears to listen for the sound of the Universe, resonating from deep within me. There is no end; if there is an end, I delve within myself to discover it. Then I open my senses to the world around me—listening to the leaves, smelling the linden trees, watching the shadows, and seeking their wisdom whenever I need guidance.

However, don't interpret this as advice; I share thoughts I've gathered from others. With closed eyes, I journey deep into my soul, searching for an ending. In that quest, I neither saw an end nor recognized myself, but I found you waiting for me and others searching for the same thing. Together, we uncovered a new alphabet.

CHANCE

The days became longer. Although all days are equally long regardless of the season, some days are long not only seasonally but also because of the rewards they offer. These were such days— generous in the sunshine and generous in offerings springing from the trees, from the streets showered by sunrays and dancing shadows, from beaches, from the faces of people.

On one of these days, I met her. Serenity bloomed in the outer place, and inside my head, I felt some knowledge and understanding that only bliss can teach; I felt her presence before noticing her in front of Gibson's. (I found her because she was waiting for me in those gloomy days, shining through the grim thoughts, making gloomy days and moods bearable.)

Then I saw her. She smiled, and we easily walked into a long day as if we knew each other or were forcibly separated and united again by a chance we had taken long before it arrived.

EVENING BY THE LAKE

That evening reminded me of a story I had imagined long ago, not so much in words but visions of a house by the lake. The gardens were not as precisely manicured as the French ones, yet they were more elegant. These visions recurred occasionally, and I couldn't tell if they reflected a lost reality, future bliss, or simply daydreams. For years, I tried to suppress them, believing they were distractions from the real world. Yet, I wanted to cherish them because I never fully understood reality, and I felt that deeper beauty and truth are not measured by the obvious or our usual perception.

It seemed as if the entire day had prepared me for this special evening when I finally confronted the reality of the visions that had always seemed unreal and too blissful. I was invited to dinner by the parents of a woman I had recently met, and the evening had finally arrived.

From the moment my car passed through the gates, I experienced an uncanny feeling of déjà vu, recognizing elements of my visions in the path leading to the house, in the trees, in the gardens, and, above all, in the white house by the lake, complete with an elegant white fountain spraying water into the air. I heard the same birds singing that had appeared in my visions, and I saw the same impeccably dressed people strolling by the fountain.

Many guests were invited, leaving me surprised. Was this all mere coincidence, or was I undeservedly honored?

The lady of my dreams greeted me first and showed me around the place I already knew. As we moved to the lake, I felt a sense of familiarity at each step. I expressed my gratitude and complimented her on the beauty of the surroundings, but I did not reveal the secret that had remained unresolved for so long.

I remembered, as if I were a ten-year-old child waking from a dream, promising not to tell anyone about it or even attempt to interpret it. I considered it an omen—a precognitive dream. I decided to wait as long as necessary to discover whether it was a reality waiting for me or merely an illusion born from desire. I learned how to find happiness either way, knowing that I had been enriched by the experience, which I considered authentic. It stayed with me as something more profound than my real experiences. I believed there had to be hidden value in it, if for no other reason than its capacity to nourish my soul for years with untranslatable beauty.

That place felt like something from another world, visiting our sometimes blind reality. I don't know if the place had been waiting for me all those years or if I was the one waiting for it. Nonetheless, I tried to learn to live in it as if it were my birthplace, accepting it as the forgotten place of my origin.

ANCIENT ROMAN VILLA

Here lies a once-splendid ancient Roman villa now in ruins. Remnants of a beautiful mosaic—depicting Venus and a flying dove—adorn the floor, while the remains of expansive gardens, fountains, and pools speak of its vibrant history. The wealthy Roman patrician who built this villa did not consider the future observers who would admire his creation. He constructed it for posterity, hoping to outlive his masterpiece. He believed he could deceive the relentless ruler, Time. Though there was no true stock market during that era, he had his treasury, which he thought would last even longer than his villa, providing wealth, power, and fame for his descendants. We can almost hear the water that once splashed from the fountains and the laughter and whispers shared among his children and servants in the gardens. We can imagine his demeanor during the extravagant parties he cherished, including the bacchanalia held in the villa's secret rooms. This ancient Roman villa lies in ruins today, and little is known about its once larger-than-life owner and even less about his fortune, treasury, and descendants.

SORRENTO

In a dream, my ideal woman chose Sorrento, on the Amalfi Coast, as the perfect place to forget the rest of the world and enjoy the endlessly beautiful Tyrrhenian Sea and its Sun. We envisioned the passage of time and listened to the sea's whispers, which held stories of lovers, travelers, strangers, and sailors eagerly sharing them with us.

As we wandered through the Piazza Tasso, we felt we were disappearing in time and space, consumed by the Mediterranean spirit. In that moment of revelation, we began to see the world in a new light. We listened to history while gazing at the sea.

In dreamy and mystical Sorrento, emerging from the sea, the plants and trees shared their stories too—lemon, agave, palm trees, pomegranate, figs, and ancient olive trees—each having witnessed countless affairs and tears throughout the years in Sorrento.

THE POETRY OF A CAR ACCIDENT

"In my deliberate opinion, the traditions of Montenegro, now committed to his Highness as a sacred trust, exceed in glory those of Marathon and Thermopylae and all the war traditions of the world."

– *William Ewart Gladstone*

Our car broke down along a snowy road in the mountains of Montenegro long before mobile phones existed. We felt like a black dot on an endless white expanse, freezing as we waited for someone or something to happen.

Maria, a wise woman who avoided taking chances, pulled two blankets from the bag. I complimented her foresight, knowing how much she appreciated compliments. Her face lit up.

Other cars passed sporadically, and as Maria began to panic, a young man finally stopped, nearly sliding down the slippery road as he walked toward us to offer help. We left our car and followed this stranger to escape the freezing conditions.

This wasn't our first experience of a similar kind. We had learned that the best people help others, even strangers, while the worst often struggle to help themselves. We understand that we should not worry about the selfishness of many because, in the end, they punish themselves more than they hurt others.

Help can be almost accidental, just as rewards often come when we least expect them, whether in a silent snowy field, on a sunny beach, or through our children passing on traditions. True goodness can arise only from good deeds.

After the stranger left, Maria asked, "Isn't he a poet?" I replied, "Of course he is." We realized poetry exists in books, verses, and unpredictable situations and places. Some of the best poets never use words; their poems are in their actions, without any desire for reward or fame, driven solely by a strong desire to help. Isn't the whole purpose of poetry to unite souls in an ongoing conversation, keeping the torch of connection lit despite any barriers?

A GOOD MAN

"The world would be much better if everyone were like you," his mother often told him. Even some of his friends shared this sentiment, but he always struggled to understand why it had to be that way. Whose fault was it that life was so complicated, and why did everything seem so difficult when he considered himself straightforward?

As time passed, and after experiencing many failures, he realized that the games of life are not simple. There is only an appearance of law, civility, and order. Like other animals, humans use everything at their disposal to fight and win in various ways, often to maintain the façade of legitimacy.

Ultimately, he concluded that the world would not be better if everyone were like him; it might perish before its time. There could be a lack of friction to keep life moving; without versatility, the world might be consumed by the monotony of pure goodness.

REWARD

Ideas can be squandered, just like material wealth. They stem from our emotions but are often stifled by our thoughts instead of being dismissed or altered. You cannot teach, cure, or fix anyone; you can only nurture the inner peace that comes from within. Often, people will observe you and learn from your example without you even realizing it. One day, you may notice a shift and find fulfillment in joy, experiencing an invisible success reflected in the happy faces of those who do not expect a reward. This is what we can call happiness.

REALITY

How comfortable it is, from a position of power, to forget that comfort is the most dangerous thing. It can blur the line between value and power, between vision and illusion (confessions don't help), and that's how mistakes are born. We think we know a lot about people and wars, yet despite all our words, something terrible always reminds us of our blindness. It's not simply a matter of knowledge or power; a powerful perspective can be blind to the obvious. It presents an illusion where even unrecognized pretense can be marketed as a legitimate solution. Ultimately, only what is real can endure: pretense cannot maintain blind power. Courage is far more significant than being deceived by a shallow victory that merely postpones a looming defeat.

MASTERY

We love the dangerous cliffs of mountains, winding roads, and rivers; jagged canyons and waterfalls seem most beautiful. We love the shadow of a cloud as it temporarily obscures the Sun, taking pleasure in both its presence and the cheerfulness it brings. There is something perfect to be found in the imperfect: the law keeps balance through the juxtaposition of beauty, which gains perfection through nurtured imperfection. Everything that looks too perfect is too perfect to be perfect. Real perfection is not too obvious. It requires effort while riding over the winding roads and flying to the clear sky to find the shadow of a cloud alive not long ago. That's why we love imperfect shapes in nature and works of art, looking for intentional errors as a sign of the golden key and sincerity in true mastery.

WORLD BEYOND OUR SHADOWS

Why do we love everything old? Perhaps it is because we are unsure of our tastes or because the fermentation process reveals deeper truths over time. Old things offer mystery and excitement as we seek to understand them. As we explore new territories, we encounter new characters and realize that, despite their differences, they share similar traumas, dilemmas, and questions. This connection reminds us of our roots and the beginning of our journey in learning how to learn, see more, and discover the world beyond our shadows.

THE MEASURE OF ALL THINGS

The collision of two galaxies is not a cosmic disaster but the union of two living entities coming together. If the idea of extinction troubles us too much, we should recognize that humans would not exist without the extinction of others over long periods of Earth's history. The extinction of one species paves the way for new beginnings, offering opportunities for others to emerge on the cosmic stage. The new ones may be better or worse; that is how life operates. Humans often judge what is good or bad, claiming to be the measure of all things, and they accept this claim as indisputable without considering the other non-human entities.

GUILT TRADERS

They tried to make us feel guilty, but their real aim wasn't to address our guilt or virtues but to teach us a lesson, not for our benefit, but to defeat us. Many of us accepted this guilt without questioning its validity or understanding what it truly was.

For those who are vulnerable, it's easy to accept guilt. Even the best among us can commit wrongs when provoked or when fighting against evil. Measuring guilt is not simple; it can be transferred from one person to another without anyone noticing. Guilt traders are aware of this and often manipulate it. If they fail to do so, they resort to using force and accuse the victim of an imposed guilt that must be acknowledged, whether it is recognized or not. If the victim is found innocent, there is no triumph—the defeated must also be considered guilty. Ultimately, it's the appearance that matters above all.

THE SILENT SCREAM

I always wondered why I never began a poem with the letter "O." I realized it was because my Os would have to be elongated, and a prolonged O would occupy the entire line. It's not a whisper; it's a scream.

THE SCIENCE OF ART

He mastered one of the most challenging arts: listening even when there is nothing to hear and conjuring vivid images from his imagination. He realized that the world is merely an echo of nothingness. True learning is elusive because nothing can be taught. Sounds are no more real than silence, so he embraced silence. The most challenging art is listening—even when there seems to be nothing to hear, allowing for the creation of vivid visions in the mind. The world is simply an echo of nothingness, and genuine understanding is unattainable since nothing can truly be taught. Sounds hold no more reality than silences.

WILDERNESS

He ventured into the wilderness to forget himself, but in doing so, he lost touch with the old world. He learned the language of wild animals, which shared their secrets with him. He became a priest of the animal kingdom.

Later, he ventured into the mountains to seek solitude and rediscover the lost world. However, he only confronted the forgotten world from a hut at the mountain's peak. Everything seemed trivial from that vantage point, and it felt like the whole world was lost in the wilderness.

BIG HEAD

A long time ago, I painted a massive head on a large sheet of drawing paper. The head seemed to hang like a rock, resembling a planet with a wide-open mouth. Its enormous teeth appeared almost ready to leap out of the watercolor.

Inside the head was a sea; within that sea, a lonely swimmer fought for his life—or perhaps for something beyond life itself. He longed to escape, but his teeth kept him captive.

I hung the watercolor on the wall, surrounded by other paintings, and this head confronted me every day for a year or perhaps even several years. Despite my daily observations, I couldn't help the man in the sea.

Eventually, I decided to remove the watercolor from the wall and destroy it.

PROMENADE

Often, I would sit on the terrace of a hotel next to the Promenade (hence its name, Promenade) in the city where I was born. I watched the people passing by and often wondered who would walk along this Promenade, leading into the central town square fifty years from now. Many years later, I can see the answer to what was lost on the Promenade.

THE SCHOOL OF THIEVES

There are typically more students than teachers. However, outside schools, in life, there are more teachers. Is this a problem of balance or a form of collective psychosis?

Everyone wants to preach, even though they claim they are only teaching. While some may occasionally offer free lessons, most impose significant fees on students who wish to learn how to navigate life more effectively.

Essentially, people are learning how to teach—or to become elite teachers, even coaching other educators. This represents an advanced level of instruction, where educators recognize that superior instructors charge higher fees and are willing to pay a premium for knowledge. They believe every experience is an opportunity to learn, but they have realized that preaching is far more profitable than genuine learning.

Consequently, they have stopped learning how to teach or preach, depending instead on their students' budgets and circumstances. The school has expanded tremendously because nearly everyone has taken at least a few classes there. Yet, it is now experiencing a marked decline in student enrollment, with the looming possibility that soon there will be no more students. This decline arises from an overwhelming focus on how to become a teacher.

Authentic learning has diminished; what remains is only the knowledge of teaching. Over time, teachers have become students of other teachers, and those educators have begun to learn from their students. This cycle has continued, with students becoming students of other students.

The structure of the school has become so intricate and sophisticated that even the original teachers have forgotten the complexities of their nearly perfect educational Ponzi scheme. No one can distinguish between a teacher and a student, nor can they discern the entrances from the exits anymore. In this situation, everyone has taken on the role of teacher, while the role of student has disappeared. Ultimately, more earnest and dedicated young learners chose to take matters into their own hands.

ALIENS I

Aliens from one planet discovered another planet with advanced beings and attacked it. They bombed and destroyed cities and countries, causing devastation and loss of life among aliens on another planet. The violence was brutal and efficient, with aliens killing their counterparts with ease. Subsequently, the invaders established a new civilization on the ruins of the former inhabitants' planet.

However, the new civilization, faced with many challenges like famines, plagues, tsunamis, earthquakes, and volcanic eruptions, slowly disintegrated and could not survive in different climates. Additionally, conflicts arose among the newly formed countries, leading to wars similar to those in the past. The new cities, just like their predecessors, bombed and attacked each other, resulting in further destruction and loss of life as if they were still the same aliens from the previous planet.

ALIENS II

An alien civilization came into contact with a much less advanced civilization. The more advanced civilization helped the less advanced one, which could hardly believe its luck. However, one day, the less advanced aliens observed that their God was guiding the advanced aliens as they worked to assist them, just as the advanced aliens had aided them.

Curious, the less advanced aliens asked if their help was due to the guidance of their God. The advanced aliens confirmed that this was indeed the main reason. They explained that, in ancient times, they had encountered other civilizations but chose not to help them; instead, they bombed, blasted, and conquered those worlds. Unfortunately, none of the planets they subdued survived for long—after brief periods of glory and prosperity, they invariably perished.

Fortunately, everything changed when they encountered a new civilization from another planet. This new civilization was more advanced than their own, causing the less advanced aliens to feel fear, weakened by eons of fruitless conquests and their vices. They were convinced they would share the same fate as their many victims throughout the Universe. Yet, the new alien civilization did not attack; instead, they extended a hand and offered their knowledge.

When the less advanced aliens asked why they chose not to destroy them, the newcomers replied that they did not use their power to spread seeds that would not grow, but rather to spread seeds that would flourish almost everywhere.

As a result, the less advanced aliens advanced so significantly that they could hardly recognize themselves as they prayed to their visitors, whom they revered as gods, even though those visitors never claimed to be such.

ALIEN RATS

A unique group of alien rats survived in a distant, unnamed galaxy after the atomic war. They discovered that a small number of the aliens responsible for the nuclear war had also survived alongside them.

EPIGRAMS, APHORISMS, AND THOUGHTS

Tradition can often feel burdensome, but without it, we would almost overnight transform into savages.

*

Tradition serves as both a powerhouse and a lighthouse.

*

Classical works and the classical world may seem daunting and demanding; however, our world, built on the foundations of the classical, can always find inspiration and guidance within it.

*

The highest levels of beauty often seem almost unattainable.

*

Genius is an inherent quality rooted in sincerity, whereas mastery is attained through hard work and dedication.

*

Not every climber can ascend the highest peaks.

*

*

The abundance in the Universe functions as an engine rather than a source of welfare.

*

Advocating for human rights does not always equate to advocating for the well-being of humanity.

*

Not all humans are equal, and not all rights carry the same significance.

*

Everyone has the right to express themselves, yet not everyone can be heard, even in the most democratic societies.

*

*

Who would truly possess knowledge if we all claimed to know everything?

*

We can all strive to learn and create; however, recognition and understanding are not always guaranteed.

*

Many experimental artists misunderstand that the world's cacophony should be replicated or mimicked in art.

*

If any notion of greatness exists, it transcends conventional greatness.

*

Winning by any means necessary is the ultimate goal of a modern savage.

*

Power and prestige are often upheld more effectively through decorum and appearance than through merit.

*

Ayn Rand overlooked that the ideal individual she envisioned can easily be supplanted by an autocrat or a cruel, though intelligent, entrepreneur.

*

A key characteristic of greatness is generosity.

*

Even if we do not strictly discuss selfishness, we must acknowledge the significance of compassion.

*

Being constrained by artificial equality is bad; neglecting the questionable sources that foster individual power or wealth is equally harmful.

*

When considering successful entrepreneurs, we often overlook that power and wealth are not always achieved through exceptional intelligence or skill, but through factors independent of personal merit.

*

It is much easier to destroy an entire city than to build a single temple!

*

Consider the passion required to create compared to the hatred needed to destroy.

*

Millennia of achievements can vanish in an instant because of hate.

*

Ultimately, hatred will consume itself if there is no one left to hate.

*

Eternal peace resides deep within us, but discovering it often necessitates a long journey.

*

There is often more happiness in a warrior fighting for his own life than in a half-alive bystander living in comfort.

*

Thinking cannot replace action, and action cannot replace thinking.

*

There is no replacement for deliberate action.

*

The invisible value of thoughtfulness is efficient when old wisdom, gained through reflection, helps us in seemingly unrelated situations.

*

What we achieve through effort often carries more significance than what we stumble upon.

*

Discoveries are earned rather than being a matter of chance, except in rare cases.

*

Kindness in your heart defines your worth as a human being, while your IQ indicates your expertise and social standing. When both are present in equal measure and accompanied by good health, there is little more to expect from life.

*

If your worth is measured only by your Ferraris, luxury homes, jets, and yachts, you are a pitiful person who deserves compassion rather than envy.

*

The more you contribute to the world, the more valuable you become.

*

Even unrecognized efforts can have an unseen impact on others.

*

It is better to die than to live as if you are already dead.

*

Soaring inward is preferable to crawling outward.

*

Different perspectives among us and our fellow human beings do not create alienation; instead, they present a greater potential for connection than artificially induced relationships.

*

Open space among people fosters a meaningful life by instilling hope for genuine unity and intimacy with others.

*

Sometimes, expressing something everyone knows but struggles to articulate is key to creating great literature.

*

It doesn't matter where the end lies; there is no true end, only existence.

*

There are genuine histories, memories, and words recorded on paper, each with varying degrees of accuracy and validity, which we collectively refer to as history. However, we often overlook how fortunate we are to have access to this knowledge; without it, we would be lost in time and disoriented, much like savages.

*

There are religions, and there is faith.

*

I don't love; I burn.

*

Hope without love is despair.

*

It was love at first sight; the issue was that it was late at night.

*

She said, "I love you," but then she took the first taxi and left with a taller man.

*

We loved each other, but she didn't share my dreams.

*

I love her, but I know how to express that to her.

*

"Love me, and I will love you" sounds like a solid business proposition.

*

She loved me, but ultimately didn't love my bank account.

*

I am careful with my finances to ensure that love stays secure and can thrive.

*

She said, "You would be a king with me." He replied, "I would be myself with you or without you. And even if I were a king but had to lose myself to gain that title, what would a king be without me?"

*

Prenuptial agreements are beneficial and essential for anyone confident in their true feelings and who appreciates variety.

*

We believe in love, but let's prioritize protecting our assets if love wanes.

*

Love is love, but business is business.

*

When people say love is in the air, they often imply that trouble is also present.

*

When someone claims to be in love, they might be feeling confused.

*

"We loved each other, and we knew why. I don't understand why we are not together," he said.
"We knew why we loved each other; that's why," she replied.

*

Love and hate are not just feelings; they are expressions of disturbances in the brain.

*

There are things I understand, some I don't, and others I love without fully comprehending.

*

People often contemplate greatness; however, nothing surpasses nothingness.

*

I believed I had discovered an answer to the question of the world's origin, only to realize it was the origin of my thoughts.

*

The greatest heroes understand that they could win but choose to lose so that others can triumph.

*

We rarely think about ants, but are very concerned with God, even though God is present in all the little things we often overlook. It's no wonder that God seems so remote and abstract.

*

I recommend writing not to those who learned how to write, but to those who discovered it unexpectedly—or from the sea when the sky is filled with clouds.

*

To be or not to be is not a question of life and death but a confirmation of both.

*

If hard work were the key to making money, mine workers would be the wealthiest.

*

There is no guilt in treason or cheating; there is only a weakness of character.

*

Lawyers effectively advocate for their clients' interests, which is why many criminals remain at large.

*

To be killed by injustice is better than being saved by justice, which kills.

*

Doctors genuinely care about the well-being of others, especially that of their affluent patients.

*

The government may be perceived as a refined form of enslavement; in extreme cases, it functions as a prison with benefits.

*

Leaders do not just fight to win votes; they engage in battles to benefit those who vote.

*

There is always something left unsaid, and there is always something left unlived.

*

Often, the unsaid is not a matter of suspense or great mystery but simply a lack of experience.

*

God is great; however, no one has ever seen or heard Him.

*

When reflecting on God, we rely on the accounts of a few and must trust their narratives.

*

There is a God that everyone observes every day—the World. However, if all eyewitnesses boasted about it, the planet would become a sanatorium.

*

This idea could be viewed as a scientific truth if we accept that God is everything and is present in everything. However, we often comprehend more through language than through a visible representation of God.

*

I have trained myself to dream, which is how I know I am not asleep.

*

Big words are generally high in volume and low in frequency.

*

I cherished the days spent relaxing on the beach, free from heavy thoughts.

*

There is almost always something good in bad situations—at least something valuable to learn.

*

We all originated from the same place, but before returning to that place, we should preserve our individual spaces.

*

He excelled in short trading and gained popularity in transient circles and networks that preferred shortcuts.

*

He participated in numerous questionable activities to rise to the top. Now, he operates a charity that allows him to sleep better at night.

*

A lie isn't a lie unless it is discovered. Even when caught on tape, it can be reinterpreted as forgetfulness.

*

Almost nobody lies, but nearly everyone has a short memory at times. That is why short memories are often the dearest to us.

*

I am curious whether you are good or bad, and I will not take your word for it.

*

In the past, we all knew each other by our first names.

*

There is no harm in inspiring, advising, and helping people improve. Profiting from it is acceptable, but it is detrimental not to acknowledge that it is a product sale, not genuine help.

*

Genuine help should not be sold. It is either a service or a product sale if it is sold. Those who truly help others never charge for their support. Buying misrepresented products is not helpful.

*

Consider carefully before buying products that promise to boost happiness or improve the lives of others.

*

There is something abject and insulting about the technicians and salespeople who sell happiness. They blatantly imply that we are fools, claiming to know something we do not, and promising to teach us how to achieve the happiness they possess, if only we subscribe.

*

When I think of gurus, the first word that comes to mind is "trick."

*

How many self-improvement books could Thoreau, Walt Whitman, Herman Melville, Emerson, and Emily Dickinson have sold if they had decided to write them? We need not mention figures like Mother Teresa or others of that ilk.

*

This is nothing new but worth repeating: true writers live for writing and, if fortunate, make a living.

*

All genuine practitioners of any art or craft live for what they do, not merely from what they do. They never sell happiness and are justly compensated for their sincere efforts, never misrepresenting their work.

*

I listen to people, but I learn from the disasters they create.

*

As long as you have wings, there is nothing wrong with being highly ambitious. Otherwise, you may end up with broken limbs.

*

Politics can be a clever way to profit from the art of lying. It can also serve as a remedy for something that would otherwise be considered an incurable illness.

*

He was a capable general—he saved the soldiers but lost the country. In contrast, another general lost many soldiers yet saved the country, leaving the remaining soldiers with vast territories to explore.

*

When emotion is absent, there is no space for ideas or deep thoughts.

*

He was an extraordinary man, yet he claimed many lives.

*

Sometimes I think morning is my favorite part of the day; other times it's evening. Occasionally, the best part is when I sleep and am unaware of my existence.

*

Great thinkers are not necessarily those who think deeply, but rather those who think easily and effortlessly.

*

He had a brilliant idea, yet no one wanted it.

*

Thinking of all the beautiful places often brings sadness about our limitations.

*

Learning to write well is possible, but teaching creativity is not. Writing skills alone are insufficient for mastery; true mastery involves much more than that.

*

We all know that we will die; yet, we continue to save things for better days until the very end.

*

The world also dies when you die, though neither seems to notice.

*

It is sad to recognize our mortality, but it becomes even more tragic when we deceive ourselves into believing we are immortal.
*

People often use "OK" as a subtle form of polite cursing.
*

Evil can arise from goodness that has become complacent.
*

Glory should be awarded to all small things.
*

Huge things obstruct the beautiful view.
*

Don't be angry at others; it's not their fault you didn't hear the clock ring early in the morning.
*

Seize the day before it comes.
*

My thoughts may be unsettling; however, they reflect the outside world from a unique perspective.
*

Being a slave to beauty means mastering the art of beautiful living.
*

Not having complete knowledge and understanding is a major source of happiness.
*

Nietzsche believed that one day everyone could achieve greatness like his own. In contrast, Whitman didn't think everyone could reach the same level of greatness, although he expressed more love and admiration for failures than for supermen or overmen.
*

We will be doomed if we continue to believe that the world began with humans and will have no end.
*

Imagination holds value as long as it stays grounded.

*

There is often more suitability in the bad than in the good. This paradox may seem irreconcilable, but it creates a necessary balance. If the opposite were true, there would be no room for either good or bad.

*

We love the truth so much that we often prefer to die rather than admit it.

*

It is impossible to understand everything; we can only wonder.

The meaning of life is to live.

*

Where are the deceased who once occupied so much space and caused so much harm? They are now in a place where they possess all the space, wealth, and peace, and do not need to steal it from others.

*

Beauty is the most generous temptress and deceiver.

*

Thinking big while using few words is a special art, yet mastering it can be challenging.

*

I love everything and nothing equally because everything would be meaningless without nothing.

*

Nothing can be said about departures except that each has a lengthy history.

*

Thinking is beautiful, but feeling is even more appealing.

*

Crying encompasses much of life, whereas words that seek attention through crying lack artistry.

*

What is believable is often as unbelievable as the incredible.

*

We often say, "This is my day and my life," although we cannot be certain if it is true.

*

Nothing is more pretentious than trying to be someone else.

*

The easiest way to gain popularity is by using superficial words, while the most complex way is to speak the truth.

*

The most painful discovery is often the truth, especially about ourselves.

*

Attempting to express something at any cost suggests a deficiency in conveying meaningful content.

*

Conveying much with few words demonstrates generous frugality.

*

"Don't underestimate me," said intelligence. "I don't," replied stupidity; "I just try to take advantage of your goodness."

*

It is unfortunate to be excessively good.

*

It is better to be slightly bad yet still good than to appear so good that one becomes unrealistic.

*

My emotions resemble a rollercoaster, but I consistently find myself grounded.

*

When you're feeling emotional, listen to some music.

*

"Don't ever come back again," she said with the same intensity and conviction for the hundredth time.

*

The sky remains blue when the clouds dissipate from our thoughts.

*

We loved each other; or at least, we believed we did.

*

Soaring high is great, but we must know how to land safely when we return.

*

Overanalyzing victories can often be worse than failing.

*

There isn't much more to say about love; it continues to endure despite the words that surround it.

*

We don't need masks; our faces serve that purpose—each is a multitude of masks.

*

"It's a beautiful day," said one ant to another as they went to work.

*

Realizing that all the hard work was futile was a significant revelation.

*

Focusing less on impressing others and more on living fully is better, yet it is hard. Still, making a positive impression on others without diminishing ourselves or anyone else allows us to embrace life fully.

*

Impressing others solely for the sake of it is not impressive. However, impressing others through thoughtfulness is beneficial.

*

Sometimes, the best remedy is to take a break from the world.

*

Feelings can be overwhelming, especially when the music is too loud.

*

Evil thoughts come from obsessing over others.

It's easy to romanticize the Good Old Days if we overlook the negative aspects.

*

Being happy doesn't require constant self-reflection.

*

Will we ever comprehend the profound difference between a king and a beggar?

*

There is no distinction between big and small; only signals in the brain exist.

*

He was so confident that he ignored his steps as he walked, even disdainful of the idea of looking down. One day, he misstepped, fell, and never rose again.

*

We can never deceive time; we can only deceive ourselves.

*

When people make mistakes, it is not the fault of time but rather an error of existence or feeling lost.

*

"Beauty lies in the eye of the beholder." Perhaps the world appears most beautiful to those who are nearsighted.

*

I have learned the most from that which has never been said.

*

When I look into your eyes, I see the world; when I gaze at the world, I see you.

*

A woman is most beautiful in our dreams.

*

While I dream, I realize that the world is alive.

*

She was beautiful but lacked a certain quality that would make her whole.

*

If you need to, express it.

*

Sometimes, oblivion serves as the best friend.

*

There is no better way to lose an acquaintance—and sometimes a friend—than by speaking the truth.

*

The secret behind bragging lies in latent insecurity. It highlights how much attention we need to feel important and happy.

*

Why is the world sometimes kind to the wicked and harsh to the virtuous? We all share the same world, which we do not fully understand.

*

This is how a bureaucratic brain functions: it has a solution to the problem; the only issue is that there is no problem. However, when a problem arises, someone must be hired to solve it.

*

I remember those sunsets when I believed I had seen the entire world.

*

Please don't call me for help; only contact me if you have no other options.

*

That was a lovely story we have heard many times before.

*

If you believe you are on top of the world, perhaps you should examine the structure that supports it—your mountain.

*

Intelligence is more important than beauty; character is more important than beauty; the quality of the soul is more important than beauty. But aren't all these aspects beautiful, and can beauty exist without them? This suggests that beauty is more significant than beauty, unless someone believes that only physical beauty is sufficient to define a person as beautiful. This belief is only valid for those who focus solely on appearances.

*

Avoid competing with anyone except yourself.

*

I always believe I will remember my thoughts, even if I don't write them down immediately before they escape. Finding them will always be an option, but creating new ones will be just as challenging. It is better to be diligent than merely thoughtful if we wish to communicate. If we focus solely on pleasure, we can do so without worrying about fleeting thoughts and oblivion. In the end, it will make almost no difference.

*

We often try to learn how to live while neglecting the essential survival skills, and vice versa.

*

We suddenly feel old and tired. Exercise and healthy food do not significantly lessen the aging that results from sudden turbulence.

*

Not all doors stay closed if we whisper the right incantations.

*

Let's take a moment of silence to appreciate this evening as it gradually unfolds.

*

We love to help others, yet we only try to impress them.

*

She loved me, and I loved her, but she didn't understand my financial situation. She was beautiful but didn't feel the same way about me.

*

A young man asked an older man, "Do women look better in short or long skirts?" The older man replied, "From my experience, naked women look the best."

*

Boredom can be a persistent issue and, in extreme cases, may be insurmountable.

*

Life consists of what we can and cannot see; often, the invisible is much more substantial than the visible.

*

Ugliness teaches us about the true value of beauty.

*

Dreaming is as essential as living.

*

Striving to reach for the sky reflects love for our original home.

*

True love can withstand anything.

*

Gentleness that results in weakness cannot be considered true gentleness.

*

Discipline imposes limitations that create true power and freedom.

*

Freedom without restraint may lead to the worst form of enslavement.

*

Our dreams reflect our identity.

*

If you want to adapt to a new world, spend at least a few months in the forest with wild animals.

*

Delve deeply to uncover the vast, undiscovered space within yourself.

*

People enjoy talking, but the issue lies not in speaking but in the inability to convey meaningful content.

*

Millions are captivated by the information they receive from television, newspapers, or the Internet, often unaware that much of it is trivial.

*

Many people speak not to communicate but to impress. Although they may sound eloquent, their words lack real impact and often serve to distract the masses.

*

We should avoid empty phrases, regardless of how polished or scholarly they sound.

*

Acquiring knowledge is straightforward, but engaging with substance is difficult.

*

Find a book or dust off one that has been neglected on your shelf.

*

Engage in conversations with people who have no need to deceive you, as their friendships will come without hidden costs.

*

Civility and politeness are often only a step away from barbarism and savagery.

*

Everything we create can be lost—not only because of natural disasters or wars but also due to indifference, apathy, a lack of compassion, and poor character.

*

We often try to teach and help others while overlooking our own need for assistance, which may be even greater.

*

If you value your life, you are successful.

*

Sincerity is vital for a genius to succeed.

*

Courage is not as rare as it may seem; there are likely more courageous people than cowards. What is truly rare is heroism.

*

Tests cannot accurately measure intelligence. We rely on tests and degrees solely because we find it difficult to trust our judgment when evaluating others.

*

What we desire is not only freedom but also peace and respect.

*

Many friendships stay strong because they have never encountered challenges.

*

Success often seems different when seen from afar. Life should not be measured solely by challenges but by our accomplishments and merits.

*

Those who lie often harbor feelings of self-hatred.

*

Disrespecting others shows a lack of self-respect.

*

We will never discover everything; therefore, we continue living and striving for more.

*

Our biggest challenge is not uncovering the secret of life's origin but the struggle for survival.

*

Much of our struggle focuses on survival instead of seeking meaning.

*

No politician or executive understands how deeply indebted they are to figures such as Archimedes, Plato, Newton, Pascal, Descartes, Kant, and others of a similar nature.

Let's seek out a thousand Newtons, especially considering the number of balloon makers that have emerged in just a few years in countries like China and Russia. Our grasp of reality seems diminished. If Buffett had not been such a modest individual, society might have mistakenly perceived him as more significant than Walt Whitman, Edison, or Tesla.

*

We often overestimate the capabilities of successful entrepreneurs. Do we think that minds like those of Tesla or Newton are incapable of achieving what individuals such as Bill Gates or Paul Allen have accomplished? Perhaps some of the most successful entrepreneurs would acknowledge that they are not irreplaceable, while minds like Shakespeare's or Einstein's are much rarer.

*

In the business world, even the most successful individuals are replaceable. The stories about their sophistication and irreplaceability are often mystifications designed to secure extremely high salaries and bonuses.

*

Business is not a science; rather, it is a skill that does not require genius. Most of all, it requires access to capital and strong organizational abilities.

*

Emotions and thoughts in people's minds and hearts constantly fluctuate between love and hate, encompassing everything in between. Mastering these emotional states requires an understanding of the sources of our joy and despair.

*

Although we cannot achieve happiness solely through our choices, making wise decisions can lead to a better life, which fosters happiness.

*

Lack of love, depression, and lawlessness exist at all levels of society. However, the lower we descend on the societal ladder, the more prevalent these issues become, both in number and intensity.

*

Nothing is easy for good reason. If everything were easy, the world would be filled with boredom.

*

God did not create the world; He is the world itself.

*

We do not need stimulus packages; we need stimulating ideas and actions. Every package incurs a cost to someone or something. Genuine stimulus not only postpones disaster but also creates real solutions.

*

To be realistic means accepting that mud is the ultimate criterion. In truth, reality is rarely more genuine than dreams.

*

Love without tension or excitement can feel too flat. That is why many relationships die from monotony.

*

A religious belief is more infectious than any physical disease.

*

How much wealth can be found in a speck of the universe like our Earth?

VIGNETTES

TIME AND SPACE

TIME: I am Time.

SPACE: You are nothing.

TIME: If I am nothing, what are you?

SPACE: I am nothing, too.

TIME: How do you know I am nothing if you are nothing?

SPACE: I know what I am; without me, you are nothing.

TIME: If you are nothing, why do I need you to become Something? If we are both nothing, then two nothings are still nothing. We both need Something; we do not need each other. Nothing cannot create love from nothing; we need Something beyond ourselves.

SPACE: Then find it. But you will not find it anywhere.

TIME: It must be somewhere; there must be something. There cannot be just two of us—two nothings; there must be Something between us or beyond us.

SPACE: What is it, then? It is nothing, too. That's why you cannot find it. You and that something are nothing without me; without me, you are dead.

TIME: You are dead, too. If you are nothing, you must be dead. Something is at least Something, and you are dead nothing. But Something is merely asleep. How can one dead revive another other dead thing? Only Something can give you life because you are nothing, and there is no life in nothing.

SPACE: You don't understand anything. To you, everything is simple and logical. Why are you nothing if everything is so simple? Why are you not always just time? Why do you introduce yourself as Time? You enjoy being young and growing old; you don't like to die.

TIME: No, I don't like to die, but you always have to die.

SPACE: I never die, but Something must always die.

TIME: Then neither you nor I ever die, just Something, Something that awakens, grows, and dies (falling asleep again).

SPACE: You are speaking now. We are nothing, but Something without us is nothing, too. Something needs space to live, to awaken; it separates at birth, creating space that needs time to measure it. Separation leads to multitudes and voyages: love affairs between Something and Nothing, creating space and Time.

Then, space and time overheard a similar conversation between Being and nothingness:

BEING: Who are you? What do you want? You have all the space, yet you are still not happy. I am small, and you are everywhere. What do you want?

NOTHING: I want to get in. I am bored, and you are bored. Let me in. Without me, you are nothing.

BEING: You are nothing. You would stay out forever otherwise.

NOTHING: You are too small; without me, you are a big zero. If I pass through you, you will grow inside.

BEING: If I am at zero, I am between two nothings; you are both inside and outside. You don't need to get in, you need to grow. I need to let you grow inside, and you should let me in. I need expansion on both sides; I let you in inside, and you let me in

70

outside. I need to pass the zero point, and you need me to fertilize you. I know you are nothing, but what am I without you?

NOTHING: Nothing.

YOU AND ME

YOU: What is new?

ME: Every day.

YOU: What is really new?

ME: Every real day.

YOU: What is real?

ME: What we think.

YOU: What do we think?

ME: What we want.

YOU: What is Love?

ME: When we soar.

YOU: Where does it happen?

ME: Anywhere.

II

YOU: What did you do today? You never tell me what you do. You are the only one who never shares. For instance: "I went to work and then had a light dinner at 'Scorpio' with a friend." You never told me this.

ME: My answer is always—nothing. I don't know why I always say—nothing. It's not that I'm hiding something; it's just that, for some reason, I say—nothing.

YOU: And you talk in riddles. You have a way of saying a lot while saying nothing. It tires my brain and drives me crazy—your riddles.

ME: Maybe that's why I always say—nothing. Maybe I don't know the answer to the riddle, and perhaps I don't want you to hear that. Perhaps the honest answer is really—nothing.

YOU: You are the one without hope or faith. I cannot cure someone who lacks hope and faith. You take life too seriously. You give the world too much power! Take the power into your hands; obviously, you don't know how to have fun.

ME: I don't know how to explain this.

YOU: You don't need to explain anything. I don't need descriptions. Just tell me: what did you do today? You can't. It's impossible for you. And you will never tell me.

ME: I think I will tell you.

YOU: But you're not telling me now.

ME: I need some time, but I promise to tell you. I know how to have fun.

YOU: I don't think you do. Outside of sex and deep conversations, you don't seem to have much of a personality.

ME: Thanks for your remark. Fun is different for different people.

YOU: That is true, but it takes a lot of intelligence to make your life fun.

ME: I agree.

YOU: You may need to loosen up a little. I like to have fun.

ME: I like to have fun too, although you may not see it.

YOU: Yeah, yeah, Mr. Conservative.

ME: Why do I like you so much if you're liberal and I'm, as you say, conservative?

YOU: Only you can answer that.

MINI ESSAYS

PROGRESS OR REGRESS

Do we ever truly understand what we owe to others and how much? We rarely think about it, almost like we were born with innate knowledge and qualifications. Acquired knowledge can be easily gained in the comfort of our rooms. However, the ideas that cultivate our knowledge emerged from hard work in the metaphorical deserts that our ancestors traversed with excruciating effort, slowly, without pretension, and often without any awareness of the actual value of knowledge, except for its purpose: to better the lives of their families and fellow human beings.

The individual who discovered fire did not seek rewards; his only motivation was the sheer joy of invention, creating something new to warm his wife and children. We still rely on the source of that first fire; we drive and fly using the power of the first wheel, constantly conquering space, often arrogantly gazing at the sky as though it were merely another resource to exploit. We attend prestigious schools and learn from knowledgeable teachers, yet many, both teachers and students, often forget their debt to those whose initial inspirations and rudimentary knowledge laid the foundation for what we now deem knowledge; without them, there would be no schools, no undeserved fame, no hubris.

Often, not those who think deeply and possess real insight who ascend the ranks, but those whose social standing and self-assuredness lead them to believe they have learned everything to know. Once they acquire knowledge, they learn how to present their thoughts as original, becoming a series of new rulers, politicians, scientists, and artists—the technicians and architects of this so-called new world, having learned in workshops. Societal issues—depressions, fears—will be addressed through the spectacle of public discourse, self-imposed podiums, and grand displays of triviality under the guise of "educating" the masses.

While monumental achievements occur in every age and every field, deserving praise and recognition, today's world often operates with minimal genuine input of innovative thought. Instead, it is driven by the techniques of technicians trained to make changes incrementally. These improvements can be misleading because they often do not represent true invention. They push us into new territories without sufficient time to reflect on the implications.

The new world can seemingly be advanced without the necessary human thought, which is precisely what we are witnessing. Computers are already solving numerous problems and will tackle even more. Progress is more misleading today than ever, as we have lost the true concept of progress. To the modern individual, progress primarily signifies comfort. Undeserved comfort, received as a gift, can be perilous. It invites laziness, both physically and mentally. This undeserved comfort relies on an illusion of absolute progress, ignoring the world's and society's cyclical nature. It fails to grasp and is incapable of understanding the concept of regress. History teaches us that regression is inevitable—a consequence of the cyclical whims of nature and society.

Why is there so little intellectual turbulence today compared to the periods of Dada, Futurism, Surrealism, and other movements? These movements, intentionally or unintentionally, reached the "end of history." Futurism was consumed by the idea of an overinflated present, where the present overshadowed the future it proclaimed. The death of a God signified not the demise of religious deities but rather the death of man's God-like aspirations. Without a divine aspect in humanity, the concept of superhuman existence, as envisioned by Nietzsche, becomes unattainable.

The myth of Icarus and its symbolic wings has been supplanted by a distorted figure like Maldoror, a creation of Isidore Ducasse (Comte de Lautréamont). The hubris of illusion and an insatiable, albeit sincere, desire to soar toward the Sun has given way to self-destructive egotism masquerading as avant-garde, perhaps not even a genuine expression. Nietzsche's conception of God diverged from that of these artists. If God is already dead, there is no justification for a second execution. Many protagonists of early twentieth-century artistic movements behaved like scavengers.

They did not recognize the fertile opportunities ahead. Instead, they sought the spotlight, securing a dictatorial role in shaping art history, often intertwined with overt or subtle political agendas. They considered themselves the vanguards, believing the future belonged to them and them alone. This mentality led to an attempt to seize it, even if it came at the expense of genuine art and literature.

Perhaps Ezra Pound was the only genuinely sincere figure amidst this cacophony of madness and perennial sadness—the fear of life. For him, the vortex idea represents the central point, the pinnacle of energy. In this regard, it served as a more authentic call for the future, captured by allure and enchantment rather than nihilism.

ARTISTIC AND SOCIAL EXTREMISM

Never before the twentieth century did artists and scientists face such disillusionment due to two world wars and other societal upheavals. Despite their good intentions to promote art, artists inadvertently contributed to what they possibly subconsciously feared was the death of art.

This was not about art for art's sake; it was about life for life's sake, with names pursued for recognition and fame rather than genuine artistic merit. Shortcuts became harmful approaches that lacked depth. Fortunately, their efforts did not wholly succeed. The outcome reflects Walter Benjamin's vision that, instead of a positive development, the result was the mass production of culture. The principle of "l'art pour l'art" was supplanted by "art for all, by all, at any time, by all means, at any price." These changes set the stage for figures like Andy Warhol, leading to a ubiquitous lowering of criteria.

A true thinker with noble aspirations was overshadowed by a speculator who made him feel ashamed of his ideals. In his desire to sacrifice his wings so that everyone could soar, he overlooked a fundamental truth: not everyone has wings, nor does everyone know how to fly. Ultimately, no one benefits from taking away the magical wings of those who seek knowledge selflessly. Pursuing equality through any means can transform the world into a barren place rather than creating a more humane and prosperous society. Those who lack wings will never take flight; if they clip the wings of those who can soar, they undermine their growth potential. The individuals who can fly have always ventured into new territories, allowing others to inhabit those spaces more comfortably.

The triumph of the educated "savage," who even contemplated the finest literature, nearly came to fruition. For a savage, there is no more enticing idea than uniting fellow savages. This was the essence of both communism and Nazism: to unify all the downtrodden, whether as the proletariat or in a nationalistic sense, ultimately undermines future progress rather than constructing it. Yet, each savage—educated or not—exists not to build but to seize what can be taken in the present, framed under the pretense of a "better future." This is, in reality, a misguided instrument of deceit and theft. That is why dogmatism and fanaticism are essential to any extremism, whether in society, politics, or art.

POETRY TODAY

At different times in history, those with something meaningful to express were compelled to write poetry or sing, unable to resist the urge. For them, it came naturally. They listened to the harmony of nature to discover their voice, and they observed other fellow human beings to understand themselves better. It was a shared struggle. Still, excellent poetry continues to be written today. Yet, many contemporary poets approach poetry as a form of healing rather than merely a necessity. This marks a new purpose for poetry. More than half of today's poets write, either for recognition or to heal their troubled souls, seeking solace in the written word when it eludes them in the world around them. We are witnessing a new era of poetry.

LITERARY FAMILY

Sometimes, I think Shakespeare is the greatest; at other times, I know it. But it sometimes feels unclear because Shakespeare never reached the highest heights of Dante's sublimity. If all philosophy is a footnote to Plato, then all literature may be a footnote to Homer. I sometimes believe Emily Dickinson is equally significant, or perhaps she reached Shakespeare's heights in a more limited scope and variety. I also see Whitman there. When thinking of Alexandria, I must also think of Cavafy and that strange feeling induced by the lands we leave behind, along with the barbarians waiting to challenge our nobility. Tolstoy must be included, as must Dostoevsky, alongside many others in this literary family. The sincerest and most profound among them were, perhaps, those least literary in a conventional sense, most natural in their expression. If one happened to be the "greatest," it was often an "accident," an outcome of being true to oneself and acting with simple, heartfelt intent. We cannot imagine Shakespeare writing so effortlessly if he had intended to outshine the Greek dramatists or if he had taken himself and his words too seriously to foresee their consequences. Such pressure would have paralyzed him. We understand that he paid special attention to the binding of his sonnets, believing this would secure his legacy, while he likely thought he would be forgotten for his plays. True greatness is, perhaps, a refusal to be great for the sake of greatness.

BOOKS CAN CHANGE THE WORLD

People often claim that books cannot change the world, similar to asserting that a New York businessperson or developer invented the formulas that underpin their business. Einstein once mentioned that he learned more about Euclidean geometry from Dostoevsky than from all the scientists combined. While books may not change the world directly, the knowledge we gain from them shapes us, and prosperity rests on the "shoulders of giants," as Newton put it. Furthermore, the unknown intellectual giants of the past often play a crucial role; influential individuals may owe more to them than to known scientists or artists. The entire framework of politics, society, and business relies on the inventions of many unrecognized individuals who pushed their imaginations to the limits, enabling others to enjoy fame and prosperity while believing they deserve the credit. Books do change the world indirectly in both visible and invisible ways.

THE ROLE OF LITERATURE IN MODERN TIMES

The role of literature in modern times is no longer the same as it was in the past. The world has changed, and as it evolves, perspectives on various activities must also adapt, causing the functions of particular arts to shift. Refusing to acknowledge the hidden requirements of our times, we neglect our responsibility to shape them following the new *zeitgeist* and emerging phenomena that demand different approaches and executions.

We do not need to point out that the role of literature is not to serve the purposes of the Epic of Gilgamesh, created over 3,000 or 4,000 years ago, nor those of Homer's epics, Virgil's works, Dante's compositions, or Shakespeare's plays, as they fulfilled needs similar to those served by television and movies today, albeit in a much nobler and more sublime manner full of catharsis.

The role of literature has changed since the 19th century, when some of the finest novels in history were written, or at the turn of the century when Proust crafted his lengthy sagas. This period predates or coincides with some of the great scientific and technological achievements of the time, which caused significant global changes in people's lives almost overnight. These transformations introduced a faster pace of living, necessitating a corresponding change in the perspective on the world and art. The new scientific era brought about a new *Weltanschauung*.

In these altered circumstances, readers are expected to tackle novels like Romain Rolland's *Jean-Christophe*, which exceeds 1,600 pages, or *Clarissa* by Samuel Richardson, comprising nearly 1,000,000 words; and even *In Search of Lost Time* by Marcel Proust, which spans 1.5 million words. Consider the modern example of Karl Ove Knausgård and his *My Struggle*, which contains about 1 million words.

Even if we recognize that many people will always be interested in the classics, we must acknowledge, given the somewhat changed role of literature today, that modern readers are less inclined to engage with extremely long sagas. In some cases, certain readers may choose their literary heroes regardless of the length of their works, but most readers will seek something less time-consuming yet not less rewarding in content and value.

Following this line of thought, Italo Calvino's short story "Black Sheep" comes to mind; its 665 words require only two minutes to read yet offer more than many lengthy novels. What can one say about Borges' "The Aleph," which exceeds 5,000 words and takes 15-20 minutes to read, yet provides more value than many extensive novels? Based on our contemporary lives, the modern reader will likely need more literature pieces like this than lengthy sagas, without underestimating the value of longer novels.

We cannot overlook the influence of Thomas Mann's novella *Death in Venice* (teetering on the edge between a novella and a novelette), which has fewer than 15,000 words, compared to almost 400,000 words in *Joseph and His Brothers*, making it about 25 times smaller than the mentioned novella.

Let's reach a consensus on these matters to navigate the modern world more effectively, considering that around 4 million books are produced yearly (half of which are self-published). Regardless of our aspirations, almost no one can read at a significantly accelerated pace; all that is valuable is necessary to understand. To streamline selective processes and help readers gain more from their reading experiences, writers and readers should adapt to changing times, enabling writers to provide more. In contrast, readers glean more by investing less time than before. This would foster a win-win scenario amidst the new challenges that literature and the arts face, competing with numerous other media and sources of influence that did not exist in the past.

ABOUT THE AUTHOR

Dejan Stojanović (1959) was born in Peć, Kosovo (formerly part of Serbia, Yugoslavia). Although he received a legal education, he has never practiced law. Instead, he became a journalist and foreign correspondent in the early 1990s; however, he is primarily a poet, essayist, philosopher, and businessman.

He has published the following poetry collections:

Circling (Krugovanje), Narodna knjiga—Alfa, Belgrade, published in three editions: 1993, 1998, and 2000.
The Sun Watches Itself (Sunce sebe gleda), NIP Književna reč, Belgrade, 1999.
The Sign and Its Children (Znak i njegova deca), Prosveta, Belgrade, 2000.
The Creator (Tvoritelj), Narodna knjiga, Belgrade, 2000.
The Shape (Oblik), Gramatik, Podgorica, 2000.
The Dance of Time (Ples vremena), Konras, Belgrade, 2007.

Pentalogy: *The World in Nowherness (Svet u nigdini),* Udruženje književnika Srbije, Belgrade, 2017:
(1) *Ozar (Ozar),*
(2) *The World and God (Svet i Bog),*
(3) *The World in Nowhereness (Svet u nigdini),*
(4) *The World and Humans (Svet i ljudi),*
(5) *The Home of Light (Dom svetlosti).*

The Hidden Light (Skrivena svetlost), Čigoja, Belgrade, 2018.
Primordial Spark (Iskra iskona), Albatros plus, Belgrade, 2021.
Centuries and Steps (Vekovi i koraci), Albatros plus, Belgrade, 2023.

Essays:
Creator and Creating (Stvaralac i stvaranje), Albatros plus, Belgrade, 2021.
The New Man and the New World (Novočovek i novosvet), Rad, Belgrade, 2022.

Anthology: *Selected Serbian Plays* (*Izabrane srpske drame*), USA, 2016.

A book of his selected interviews, *Conversations* (*Razgovori*), was published in 1999 by NIP Književna reč in Belgrade. The Serbian Heritage Foundation and the Association of Writers of Serbia for Intellectual Engagement awarded the book the Rastko Petrović Prize.

Collected Poems: 1978-2000 (Pentalogy 1), New Avenue Books, 2025 (Translation from Serbian).

Books written in English:

Philosophy: *Absolute,* New Avenue Books, USA, 2024.

Poetry Series: *The Embrace of Light and Darkness* (Pentalogy 3):
- *Dance of Sounds*, New Avenue Books, 2025
- *The Matter of Matter*, New Avenue Books, 2025
- *The Home of the World*, New Avenue Books, 2025
- *All Women in One*, New Avenue Books, 2025
- *Strange Thoughts* (prose), New Avenue Books, 2025

He lived in Chicago, USA, from 1990 to 2014, and holds citizenship in both Serbia and the United States.

www.ingramcontent.com/pod-product-compliance
Lightning Source LLC
Chambersburg PA
CBHW052014240626
47153CB00008B/2869